Under a Silver Moon

Other books by Anne Fine include:

The Diary of a Killer Cat
Care of Henry
Design a Pram
The Haunting of Pip Parker
*How to Cross the Road and Not Turn
into a Pizza*
It Moved!
Nag Club
Only a Show
Press Play
The Jamie and Angus Stories
Jamie and Angus Together
Jamie and Angus Forever
The Same Old Story Every Year
Scaredy Cat
Stranger Danger?
The Worst Child I Ever Had

Under a Silver Moon

Anne Fine

Illustrations by
Lotte Klaver

First published 2010 by Walker Books Ltd
87 Vauxhall Walk, London SE11 5HJ

2 4 6 8 10 9 7 5 3 1

Text © 2010 Anne Fine
Illustrations © 2010 Lotte Klaver

The right of Anne Fine and Lotte Klaver to be identified as
author and illustrator respectively of this work has been asserted by
them in accordance with the Copyright, Designs and Patents Act 1988

This book has been typeset in StempelSchneidler and Braganza ITC

Printed and bound in Great Britain
by CPI Mackays, Chatham ME5 8TD

British Library Cataloguing in Publication Data:
a catalogue record for this book is available from the British Library

ISBN 978-1-4063-1923-1

www.walker.co.uk

for Zachary
A.F.

for Kees and Thea
L.K.

ONE

Once, in a hot land, far, far

away, two baby boys were born under the

same silver moon.

Haroun, Lord of the Rolling Desert Sands,

Mirror of Stars and Heir to All Gifts and

Wonders, was the son of the Sultana and

Sultan. He lay in a silken cradle, and the

ladies of the bedchamber took turns to cool

him with fans. The finest singers came from

all over the land to sing him lullabies.

Akil was the son of a kitchen servant

and the head gardener, and he was put into

a basket under the kitchen table so that his

mother could get on with her work.

The sun came up and the sun went
down. Little Akil learned to walk. Then talk.
Then rush about. When he was in the
kitchen, he ran to fetch spoons and
dishes for the cooks, or another
branch of wood for the fire.

When he was in the garden, he
used a little wooden trowel
to help his father make new
flowerbeds.

Dig, dig, dig.

Sift, sift, sift.

Dig, dig, dig.

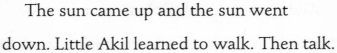

And sometimes he just ran round the fountains, watching the birds and sticking his nose in the sweet-smelling jasmine.

Mostly, Prince Haroun sat in the palace chambers, playing alone with his toys. But sometimes the ladies of the bedchamber brought him down to the garden so that they could walk under the fine rose arches that Akil's father had made, or sit whispering together under the shade of the jasmine canopies.

One day, Prince Haroun saw the boy,
who was the same age as himself,
digging at the far end of
the garden, and asked,
"Who's that?"

"He is the son of a kitchen servant and the gardener," the ladies told him.

"What is his name?" asked Prince Haroun.

"He's called Akil," they said.

"Is that all?" said Prince Haroun. "Isn't he Lord of anything, Mirror of anything, or Heir to All anything?"

"No," said the ladies. "He is just Akil."

"Well, bring him here, please," said Prince Haroun, "so I can play with him."

And because he was Lord of the Rolling Desert Sands, Mirror of Stars and Heir to All Gifts and Wonders, the ladies felt they couldn't argue. So they went to Akil's father and said, "We've come to borrow your son because Prince Haroun wishes to play with him."

Akil's father bowed and nodded. So Akil threw down his trowel and ran to play with Prince Haroun.

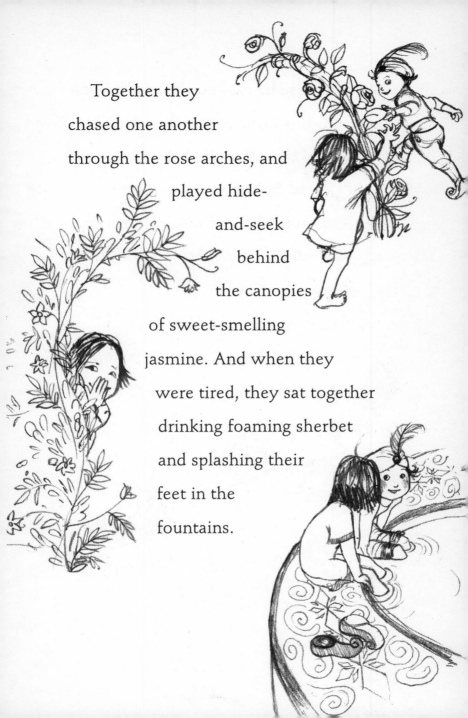

Together they chased one another through the rose arches, and played hide-and-seek behind the canopies of sweet-smelling jasmine. And when they were tired, they sat together drinking foaming sherbet and splashing their feet in the fountains.

The day went
by so quickly
that when the
ladies of the
bedchamber
took Prince
Haroun back
up the palace
steps, he told
them firmly, "I'm
going to play with Akil again tomorrow."

And nobody dared argue.

TWO

Every day after that, the two
boys played together in the garden.

As the sun rose, Prince Haroun
sat up in bed and waited impatiently
while the ladies of the bedchamber
chose one of his hundreds of silken
robes, shook out its creases and
dropped it carefully over his head.

At the other end of the
palace, Akil rolled off his sleeping
mat and tugged on the tunic he'd
rinsed and hung out to dry the
night before.

Prince Haroun sat at the marble table and waited an age while the ladies of the bedchamber coaxed him to choose from all the fancy foods piled high on golden plates and silver bowls.

At the other end of the palace, Akil grabbed a bread roll and a handful of dates, and went out into the garden.

While he was waiting, Akil helped his father. Sometimes he helped dig. Sometimes he helped plant. Sometimes he watered and sometimes he picked out weeds.

But as soon as Prince Haroun came rushing down the steps and called to him, Akil would drop his trowel or watering can and run over to play while the ladies of the bedchamber sat in the shade under the jasmine canopies and whispered to one another.

"One day," they said, "the prince will be too old to play in the garden like any other child. He will be far too busy learning to be Lord of the Rolling Desert Sands, Mirror of Stars and Heir to All Gifts and Wonders."

Sure enough, the day came when the Sultana and Sultan walked down the steps into the garden. Behind them was the Grand Vizier.

"Where is the prince?" the Grand Vizier asked the ladies of the bedchamber.

The ladies blushed and pointed, for there in one of the flowerbeds were Haroun and Akil, wriggling about on their stomachs, pretending to be giant worms.

The Sultan strode
into the flowerbed
and pulled his son
to his feet. "This is
no way to learn to be
a prince!" he said.
And, taking the
Grand Vizier aside,

he pointed at Akil, who was still brushing
the dried earth off his tunic, and told him,
"Please keep that child away from mine."

So the Grand Vizier went to Akil's father
and said, "Squirming about like a worm in
the flowerbeds is no way for your son to
learn to be a gardener."

Akil's father nodded.

And the next day, when Akil threw on his tunic and ran out into the garden with his bread and dates, he found his father waiting with two spades, two hoes and two pruning knives.

"Playtime is over," Akil's father said.

"It's time for the prince to learn how to be a proper prince, and for you to learn how to be a proper gardener. So come with me."

THREE

The sun came up and the sun went down. The months passed and Akil learned all there was to know about being a gardener. He learned how to water plants without washing them away. He learned to tell a weed from tamarisk, and coriander from a weed. He learned to make a rose arch and a canopy of jasmine, and how to trail creepers over the edge of a fountain until it looked just like a natural pool.

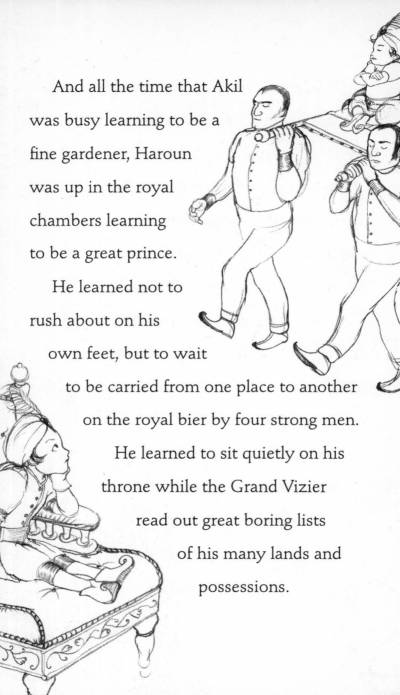

And all the time that Akil was busy learning to be a fine gardener, Haroun was up in the royal chambers learning to be a great prince.

He learned not to rush about on his own feet, but to wait to be carried from one place to another on the royal bier by four strong men. He learned to sit quietly on his throne while the Grand Vizier read out great boring lists of his many lands and possessions.

He learned to stay awake through all the long royal ceremonies and even longer royal feasts.

He learned that for everything that needed doing, there was a servant to do it. A servant to open doors, a servant to open windows, a servant to carry books or brush the crumbs from his gown, a servant to bring him water or hot towels – even a servant to pull back his bed sheet.

And since the only thing he was allowed to do for himself was lift his own food to his mouth, that's what he did.

Over and over.

For hours every day.

The sun came up and the sun
went down. Months passed, and
Prince Haroun gradually became as
round as a butterpat, then as round
as the fattest olive, and finally
as round as the moon.

And down in the garden, Akil
and his father had to widen the rose
arches and the canopies of jasmine
because the Grand Vizier had to
order another bigger royal
bier to carry the Lord of
the Rolling Desert Sands,
Mirror of Stars
and Heir to All Gifts
and Wonders.

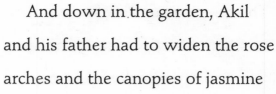

FOUR

One morning everyone in the palace was woken by a terrible howling and wailing.

Prince Haroun had pains in his belly.

Doctors were summoned, and they all agreed: "The prince must go to bed and do nothing till the pains are gone."

So Prince Haroun went to bed
and did nothing. But the pains
didn't go. They spread.

"Now my back
aches," the prince
moaned.

More doctors
were summoned. They
agreed as well: "The prince must lie on
even softer pillows."

So the prince lay on even softer pillows.
But the pains didn't go.
They spread.

"Now my knees are stiff,"
the prince wailed.

More doctors were summoned, and they
too agreed: "The prince must even stop
wiggling his toes."

The prince lay perfectly still for
three whole days.

The only bit of him that moved was
his hand as it lifted the spoon from his
dish to his mouth.

Over and over.

The pains became worse, and in the end the prince burst into tears and complained to the doctors, "Not one of you has the least idea how to cure me. Clearly I'm going to die. I want to spend my last few days beside the fountains where I spent so many happy hours playing with the son of the gardener."

Nobody felt that they could argue with him. So the Grand Vizier sent for the new, bigger, wider royal bier, and eight strong men carried Prince Haroun out into the palace garden, and set him down under the canopy of sweet-smelling jasmine that Akil and his father had widened only the year before.

FIVE

At the far end of the garden, Akil
leaned over to tug his father's sleeve.

"See? It's the prince."

Akil's father looked
up. "Poor boy!" he
said. "When the
two of you
tumbled together around
the gardens, you looked
like brothers and you were
both so happy. But some
get all the good fortune in the
world, and others all the ill luck."

Akil was baffled. "But he is Lord of the Rolling Desert Sands, Mirror of Stars and Heir to All Gifts and Wonders. And we are simply his poor gardeners."

"A man is happy," Akil's father said, "not when his riches are many but when his wants are few. We have bread and dates and spend our lives busily in the most beautiful garden. Now Prince Haroun is as round as one of the barrels of sherbet in his own cellars and you are as slim and sturdy as your own rake.

But if you two were to exchange your lives,
soon you would have his shape and pains, and
he would have your health and cheery spirits."

"Why don't the doctors tell him?" cried
Akil.

"What?" Akil's father laughed. "Dare tell
a prince to get off his feather pillows and
do a hard day's work, and then another and
another? Would you be foolish enough?
Or would you worry that he might lose his
temper and you might lose your head?"

Then Akil's father laughed again, and
walked off to fill his watering can
while Akil stared across the
garden at the unhappy prince.

Thinking and thinking.

SIX

Next day, a small man in a heavy black hood came to the door of the palace and told the Grand Vizier, "I must see the Sultana and Sultan. I have good news for them. It is a secret about the prince's sickness."

The Grand Vizier did not dare turn him away. Instead, he led him to the royal chambers. "This stranger brings a secret about the health of your son."

The Sultan grasped the hooded man by the shoulders. "Tell us at once! If there is any way to save our dear Haroun's life, then we must know it!"

The stranger smiled. "Somewhere in your palace garden," he told them, "hidden under the stony soil, there lies a magic key. A spell is on it, and the moment this key lies in your son's hand, he will be cured of all his pains."

The Sultan was ecstatic.
"Send men!" he cried. "Send
men at once to dig all over
the garden and find this key."

The stranger raised his
hand. "Wait. There is one
problem. Only the person who
finds the key can have the good
health it brings."

"What?" said the Sultana.
"Must our son dig for it himself?
With no help from anyone?"

"Well," said the stranger. "He may
take advice from his old friend Akil, the
very sensible son of the gardener. But, as for
the digging itself, that must all be his own."

The prince was told the news. He wept

and wailed. But the Sultan and the Sultana

loved him so

much that

they were

adamant.

If it would

make

him well

again,

then he must

dig for the key all by

himself, with no help from

anyone except for a little advice from his

old friend Akil, the very sensible son of the

gardener.

SEVEN

Dig, dig, dig.

Sift, sift, sift.

Dig, dig, dig.

The first day was the worst. Oh, how Prince Haroun groaned and moaned and stared at the blisters on his poor soft hands.

The second day was the
second worst. Oh, how he
whimpered and grumbled,
and pressed his hands
against his sore, bent back.

The third day was the
third worst. Oh, how he
cursed and scolded the
heavy lumps of soil he
lifted with his spade.

On the fourth day,
for just a few moments at the
start, Prince Haroun almost
enjoyed himself (till all
his blisters rose again).

On the fifth day,
the prince heard
whistling and looked
up, quite astonished,
to find the merry
noise was coming
from his own lips.

On the sixth
day, he set himself
a goal – to dig as far as
the next flowerbed – and
when he reached it, he set
himself another.

On the next day, he got up early just to get started on his task. And the day after. And the day after that. Soon, he was slipping out of the palace even before the ladies of the bedchamber could try to coax him to eat all the fancy foods piled high on golden plates and silver bowls.

Down in the garden, Akil was waiting with a handful of dates and a bread roll and (since he was not the son of a gardener for nothing) one or two fresh ideas for the garden.

"It is a shame to waste all this freshly turned soil of yours," he told the prince. "Shall we plant quinces and nectarines?"

"I thought perhaps pomegranates,"
returned the prince. "And maybe a lavender
bed in the shape of a heart to please the
ladies of the bedchamber who are so lonely
without me."

The sun came up and the sun went
down. The weeks passed. Akil's
father sat in the shade of
a tamarind tree
and smiled as he
watched the two
boys working
together in the
garden as closely
and as steadily
as once they
had played.
The prince broke up
the hard and stony soil, and right
behind him came Akil, planting
and watering, staking and

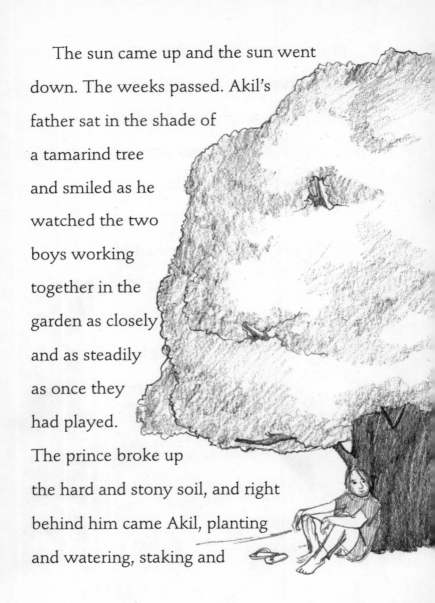

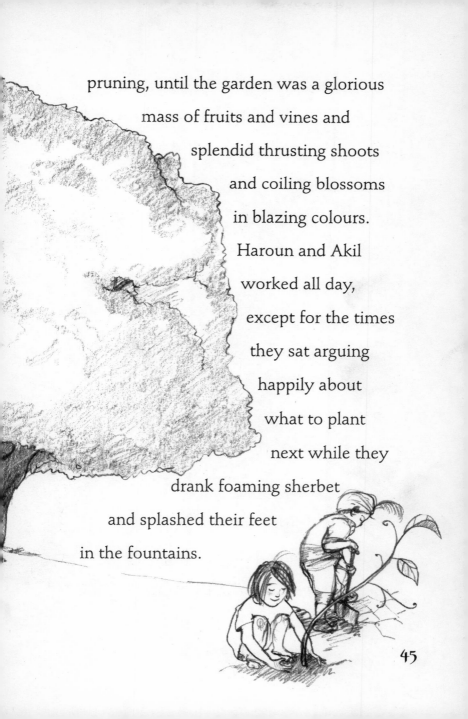

pruning, until the garden was a glorious
mass of fruits and vines and
splendid thrusting shoots
and coiling blossoms
in blazing colours.
Haroun and Akil
worked all day,
except for the times
they sat arguing
happily about
what to plant
next while they
drank foaming sherbet
and splashed their feet
in the fountains.

The sun came up and the
sun went down. Months passed.
Prince Haroun dug around the
palace gardens, to the north and
to the south, to the west and to the
east. And then, one day, he found that
he had dug the very last spadeful of
earth beside the very last of the
palace gates.

He turned to Akil. "I have
been cheated!" he declared. "That
hooded stranger was nothing but
a liar! I have dug over every
clod of this garden, and
there's no magic key."

"No magic key, perhaps," said Akil. "Yet there has been no cheating either. Nor any lies. For you have unlocked the door to your own health and happiness. Look at yourself!"

The prince looked down. And it was true! He was no longer as round as one of the barrels of sherbet in his own cellars.

He was no longer even as round as the fattest olive. He was not even as round as a butterpat. His back was straight. His arms and legs were strong. All of his pains were gone. Magic indeed!

Prince Haroun threw down his spade and strode back towards the palace.

Passing Akil's father on the way, he stopped to ask, "Gardener, do I look well to you?"

Akil's father bowed. "You have never looked better, sire. You look as strong and firm as the fruit bushes that you and my son have planted beside the west wall."

Prince Haroun hurried on. Finding
the ladies of the bedchamber whispering
together under the shade of the jasmine
canopies, he asked them, "Ladies, do
I look well to you?"

"Indeed you do, sire,"
they assured him. "As lithe and hardy as any
of the vines that you and Akil have planted
together along the south wall."

Prince Haroun ran up the steps and
called for the palace doctors. They all came
running.

"Do I look well to you?"
he demanded.

"You have never looked
fitter," they insisted. "You are as sound
and vibrant as the green shoots that spring
up wherever you and Akil have been digging
and planting in the north gardens."

Prince Haroun ran into the royal chambers and asked his mother and father, "Do I look well to you?"

The Sultana answered, "You look as fine and rosy as any of the blossoms that you and Akil have tended and watered in the east gardens."

The Sultan agreed. "My son," he said. "It seems to me that you are in perfect health."

The prince ran back to Akil, who was waiting by the garden gate. "It seems," he said, "that everyone is now agreed that I am in perfect health. Yet there is no key. So I begin to wonder about that hooded stranger..." And Prince Haroun gave his oldest friend a very long and suspicious look.

Akil just grinned. "Magic may work in strange ways," he said. "And you have certainly found the key to good health. Perhaps, even when you are the wise and powerful Sultan, we will be able to work together from time to time. Then you can add one more fresh honour to your family name."

"And what will that be?" Prince Haroun asked his friend.

Akil told him, "You can call yourself Lord of the Rolling Desert Sands, Mirror of Stars, Heir to All Gifts and Wonders – and Prince of the Palace Garden!"

"Indeed I can," said Prince Haroun. "And
so I shall. And you may add an honour to
your name as well."

"What's that?"

Prince Haroun chuckled. "You shall be:
Akil, Wisest of Hooded Strangers."

Then, laughing, the two of them raced
off to the kitchen, where Akil's mother
made them one more foaming sherbet
to share before they happily went back
to making the garden that the two
of them had created even more
beautiful than before.

Anne Fine is a distinguished
writer for both adults and children. She
has won numerous awards for her children's
books, including the Carnegie Medal twice,
the Whitbread Children's Book of the
Year Award twice, the Smarties Book Prize
and the Guardian Children's Fiction Prize. In
2001, Anne became Children's Laureate and
in 2003, she was awarded an OBE and
Fellowship of the Royal Society of Literature.
Her other titles for Walker Books include *Care of
Henry*; *How to Cross the Road and Not Turn into a
Pizza*; *Nag Club*; and the Jamie and Angus series.
Anne has two grown-up daughters
and lives in County Durham.

You can find out more about Anne Fine
and her books by visiting her website at
www.annefine.co.uk

Lotte Klaver wanted to be either a veterinarian or an illustrator when she was growing up. She chose the latter, and loves being able to draw every day. After graduating from art school, she started a drawing blog on her website www.lotteklaver.com. She exhibits her work in galleries and does illustrations for various things. *Under a Silver Moon* is her first children's book. Lotte lives in Amsterdam with her cat, Tom.

Jamie pressed his nose up hard
against the glass and gazed at Angus.
Angus gazed at him. "Oh, please,"
said Jamie. "Please."

From the moment Jamie sets eyes on Angus
in the shop window, he just knows that
they belong together. On Christmas morning
they're finally united, and soon the toy
Highland bull is Jamie's best friend.